DINOSAUR WORLD

Long-necked Dinosaurs

Robin Birch

CHELSEA
CLUBHOUSE

An Imprint of Chelsea House Publishers
A Haights Cross Communications Company

Philadelphia

Chelsea Clubhouse
1974 Sproul Road, Suite 400
Broomall, PA 19008-0914

The Chelsea House world wide web address is www.chelseahouse.com

Library of Congress Cataloging-in-Publication Data

Birch, Robin.
  Long-necked dinosaurs / by Robin Birch.
  p. cm. — (Dinosaur world)

  Includes index.
  Summary: Describes the appearance, eating habits, and habitat of long-necked dinosaurs, including Brachiosaurus, Diplodocus, Camarasaurus, Mamenchisaurus, and Anchisaurus.

  ISBN 0-7910-6988-5
  1. Saurischia—Juvenile literature. [1. Saurischians. 2. Dinosaurs.] I. Title. II. Series.
  QE862.S3 B57 2003
  567.912—dc21

                                                                        2002000841

First published in 2002 by
MACMILLAN EDUCATION AUSTRALIA PTY LTD
627 Chapel Street, South Yarra, Australia, 3141

Copyright © Robin Birch 2002
Copyright in photographs © individual photographers as credited

Edited by Angelique Campbell-Muir
Illustrations by Nina Sanadze
Page layout by Nina Sanadze

Printed in China

Acknowledgements
Auscape/Jaime Plaza Van Roon, p. 7 (bottom left), Auscape/Francois Gohier, p. 20, Auscape/Ferrero-Labat, p. 21; Australian Picture Library/© Corbis, p. 5 (top left); Corbis Digital Stock, p. 7 (top); The Field Museum (neg. no. GN86809-2c), p. 12; Gondwana Studios, p. 24; © The Natural History Museum, London, pp. 5 (bottom left), 9, 13, 16; The Peabody Museum of Natural History, Yale University, New Haven, Connecticut, p. 29; Getty Images/Photodisc, p. 7 (bottom right); Photolibrary.com, pp. 5 (top right), 25; Royal Tyrrell Museum of Palaeontology/Alberta Community Development, p. 5 (bottom right).

While every care has been taken to trace and acknowledge copyright, the publisher tenders their apologies for any accidental infringement where copyright has proved untraceable.

Contents

Dinosaurs

Dinosaurs lived millions of years ago. There were no people on Earth when dinosaurs were alive.

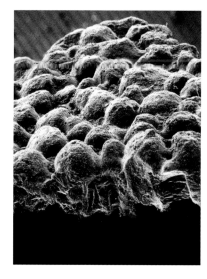

We know dinosaurs lived because people have found their bones, footprints, eggs, and **droppings**. Scientists study these **fossils**.

Long Necks

Some dinosaurs ate animals and others ate plants. Long-necked dinosaurs were plant eaters. They probably lived in forests and other places where many plants grew.

Long-necked dinosaurs could stretch to reach for ferns, pine trees, and other plants. They even ate tough pinecones.

7

Long-necked dinosaurs often lived in large groups called **herds**. Herds walked long distances to find food. Traveling in herds helped the dinosaurs protect themselves from hungry meat-eating dinosaurs.

Long-necked dinosaurs laid eggs, as all other dinosaurs did. The eggs had hard shells. Some eggs did not hatch. Over time, they turned into rock. Scientists have dug up these fossils to study.

9

Brachiosaurus

(BRACK-ee-uh-SAWR-uhs)

Brachiosaurus was one of the largest and heaviest land animals to ever walk the earth. It stood 50 feet (16 meters) tall and weighed 80 tons (72 metric tons).

Brachiosaurus had a short tail compared to other long-necked dinosaurs. Its front legs were longer than its back legs, so its back sloped downward. It had small, narrow feet.

Brachiosaurus had nostrils on top of its head. Scientists think it had a good sense of smell. It used its pencil-shaped teeth to break off plants to eat. Brachiosaurus swallowed its food whole.

Long-necked dinosaurs like Brachiosaurus
swallowed stones. The stones stayed in their
stomachs and mashed up the plants they
ate. The stones helped the dinosaurs **digest**
the food in their stomachs.

13

Diplodocus

(di-PLOD-uh-kuhs)

Diplodocus was one of the longest dinosaurs that ever lived. It had a very long neck and a very long tail.

Diplodocus had straight, thick legs. Its back legs were longer than its front legs. Each foot had five toes.

Diplodocus had **blunt** teeth that helped it strip leaves off trees. Its long neck could reach into places where its body would not fit. Diplodocus reached into forests to feed on low plants.

Diplodocus held its tail up off the ground. It could **lash** its tail from side to side like a whip to defend against attacks by other dinosaurs.

Camarasaurus

(kuh-MARE-uh-SAWR-uhs)

Camarasaurus was a small long-necked dinosaur. It had a thick body. But its neck and tail were short. Hollow spaces in its backbone made it lighter than other long-necked dinosaurs.

Camarasaurus had long front legs that were only a little shorter than its back legs. Its body was almost level with the ground. It had a strong, sharp claw on the first toe of each front foot.

Camarasaurus had a short head. It had spoon-shaped teeth for cutting and tearing plants. It probably ate tough food like twigs, bark, and branches, as well as leaves.

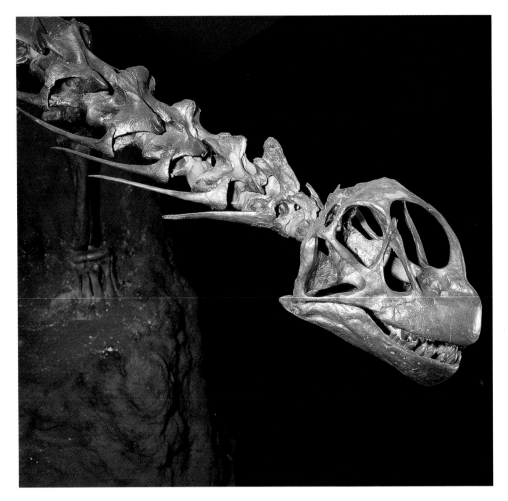

Like other long-necked dinosaurs, Camarasaurus had straight, thick legs like an elephant's.

Mamenchisaurus

(mah-MEN-chih-SAWR-uhs)

Mamenchisaurus might have had the longest neck of all the dinosaurs. Its neck stretched 46 feet (14 meters) to a small head.

Mamenchisaurus also had a very long tail.

Mamenchisaurus had teeth like pegs, with gaps between them. Mamenchisaurus might have scooped up mouthfuls of plants growing in water and let the water drain out through these gaps.

Scientists study footprints of long-necked dinosaurs like Mamenchisaurus. The animals made the prints when they walked in soft mud. The mud became hard and after many years turned to rock. These footprints are a type of fossil.

Anchisaurus

(ANG-kee-SAWR-uhs)

Anchisaurus was a very small dinosaur. It stood only 3 feet (1 meter) tall. Anchisaurus had a small, narrow head. Its teeth were shaped like a saw to help it shred plants as it ate.

Anchisaurus had legs that were longer than its arms. It might have walked on all fours, but it ran fastest on just its legs. Anchisaurus had a large, curved claw on each hand.

Anchisaurus lived near lakes. When there was no rain, the lakes dried up. Groups of the dinosaurs walked across the soft mud, leaving footprints behind.

Scientists have dug up and studied Anchisaurus bones.

Names and Their Meanings

"Dinosaur" means "terrible lizard."

 "Brachiosaurus" means "arm lizard."

"Diplodocus" means "double **beam**," which refers to the shape of the bones in the tail.

"Camarasaurus" means "**chambered** lizard," which refers to the hollow spaces in the backbone.

"Mamenchisaurus" means "Mamenchi lizard"; Mamenchisaurus was found in Mamenchi, China.

 "Anchisaurus" means "near lizard"; Anchisaurus has this name because it was related to some of the very first dinosaurs.

Glossary

beam a long, thin object used for support

blunt dull; not sharp

chamber a space inside an animal's body

digest to break down food so that the body can use it

dropping the waste matter of an animal

fossil something left behind by a plant or animal that has been preserved in the earth; examples are dinosaur bones and footprints.

herd a large group of animals that live together

lash to whip back and forth

Index